LIQUID STATUS

BRADLEY SANDS

Published by Rooster Republic Press LLC
Copyright © Bradley Sands
Cover Design by Matthew Revert

Find our catalog at

www.roosterrepublicpress.com

"This reads like what might happen if Freud and the Joker collaborated on a rewrite of Blake Butler's There Is No Year. A weird and swerving book that nonetheless says a lot about the hidden dynamics of families."

-Brian Evenson, author of A Collapse of Horses

LIQUID STATUS

LIQUID STATUS

LIQUID STATUS

LIQUID STATUS

LIQUID STATUS

LIQUID STATUS

LIQUID STATUS

This is the only house in the neighborhood without a basement. The absence has lowered its property value. Young couples do not want to live in a house without a basement. The neighborhood does not have basements of dirt, stone, furnaces, and spiders. These things have been replaced by soft carpeting, toys, flat-screen TVs, and video-game consoles. This house does not have these things. This house feels incomplete to its residents, who are sitting in the living room rather than a basement. They feel an emptiness, but cannot determine its cause.

Grandma does not feel the emptiness. She does not live in this house. She lives by herself, in an apartment building with senior citizens. She has maneuvered into the house so she can gaze at a portrait of herself from the nineteen-thirties. The woman in the portrait is very beautiful. She is more beautiful than Grandma because the years have spent a lot of her beauty on wisdom and experiences. Grandma maneuvers herself into the house once a month. She does not remember why her portrait is in this house's living room. She is too timid to request its presence in her apartment.

The family has separated into two groups. They sit on couches surrounding a coffee table. There are no coffee cups on the table. This is not allowed. Mom has decreed the living room should remain unsoiled. She does not allow anyone to sit or stand in it unless it is during one of Grandma's monthly visits. The living room has not been reserved for the living. It is a sacrifice to Mom's gods. She has offered them abstract paintings, a chessboard that has never been played, expensive picture frames with old photos inside, decorative pillows, plastic plants, and a liquor cabinet with unopened bottles.

Grandma smiles. She is smiling at the flower in her younger self's hair. A man gave her the flower after they stole a grocery cart filled with enough food to cover a picnic blanket. Her family is unaware of her romantic history of petty theft. They will never know how good the stolen food tasted or how her heartbeat sped up when she pressed against the man's body. She could try to describe it, but her words would be indefinite. She could try to describe it, but her heart stops after she feels the smoothness of his right hand.

Mom notices Grandma has become quiet, still. "Mom?" She says it louder, interrupting a conversation between Dad and one of his sons.

The living room pauses. A few seconds will need to pass before it progresses. Its contents do not move or make sounds.

Mom shakes Grandma, yells, "Mom?"

Dad stands up, walks over to them.

The brothers look at their mom. They have never heard such volume in the living room before. Such volume is against the rules. But like other rules, it is ok to break this one when Grandma comes to visit.

The dog is barking. Mom is crying. Dad says, "We should bury Grandma in the backyard so the police do not suspect foul play."

Mom stops crying. She looks at her husband, confused. "Why would you say such a thing?"

"I am not going to jail because your mother was too old to sustain her biological functions."

Mom hugs Grandma.

"It will be difficult to dig a grave for her under all this snow. Do you think she will melt in the springtime if I give her a snowy grave rather than a dirty one?"

Paul asks Dad if he has gone crazy.

Dad does not say, "No, I have not gone crazy" or "Yes, I have gone crazy." Paul did not expect a yes or no answer. This is not that sort of question. It is a question that functions as a reality check.

Dad says, "Sorry, Paul. I do not know what is wrong with me. I have never had to deal with the legal implications of death before."

Paul's younger brother, Matt, avoids the implications of death by playing chess against himself on the board. This is the first time it has known the sensation of touch.

Mom takes a break from her grief. "Just call the police, Nathan. They won't charge you with a crime. My mother has died. This is not a crime."

Dad says, "But what if there is an unexpected factor in her death that implicates one of us? What if the police can read my mind and find out about all the times I have wished for her death?"

Mom gives him a stern look.

Dad walks out of the living room, into the hallway that separates it from the front door, kitchen, and two staircases. He removes the cordless phone from its cradle. He shouts, "What is the number for the police?" His voice echoes through the hallway.

Mom says, "Just call 911 if you can't find the phone book."

"I cannot find the phone book." His jaw opens in terror. "I am afraid death is not an emergency. I think there is a law against dialing 911 if it is not an emergency."

Mom gives him a stern look.

He dials 911, looks worried, puts the phone back into its cradle, tries to call 911 on his cell phone, shakes his head, says, "The number I am trying to reach is not available at this time. It must be the storm." He dials Milligan's number, shakes his head, puts the cell phone into his pocket, says, "I do not know what to do." He runs out the front door, leaving the door open, leaving the dead grandmother to deal with the snowflakes accumulating in the hallway.

Dad returns, shaken. He closes the door. The snowflakes begin to melt. The dead grandmother stops worrying about the location of the snowflakes. They are no longer in the wrong place. She never has to worry about anything again. She is free.

Dad says, "No one is home. No one in the neighborhood is home. No one answers their doors. Their cars are in their garages, but no one is home. Every light in every house in the neighborhood is on, but no one is home. When I looked through windows, there was nothing inside. No furniture. No nothing." He dances around the room. "No furniture. No nothing. No furniture. No nothing." Snow falls out of his hair and off his clothes.

Matt says, "Checkmate." He looks out the window. He does not see any cars passing their house. All he sees is snow. He does not like cars. He likes snow. He is happy. He has not been happy in a long time. There are always cars traveling through Spruce Lane.

Mom looks at Dad with a blank expression. She looks out the window. There is nothing outside that makes her happy. The snow causes her features to curl until her face resembles a poorly-carved jack o' lantern. She feels a compulsion to leave the house. She walks out of the living room, enters the hallway, screams.

There is no front door.

444

Had there ever been a front door?

Dad removes his toolbox from the hall closet, opens it, grabs a hammer, shows the hammer to the wall where the door used to be. The wall does not frighten. He fills the wall with holes. Sunlight does not leak out of the holes. Darkness gushes. Dad stops hammering. He descends the stairs to the den. He mourns the basement.

The den has de-evolved. Before, it was a reflection of the living room as seen through a dirty mirror. Full of victims of wear and tear. A room where living was encouraged. The living room's surrogate. A room that should have been called the dying room according to driveway vs. parkway logic.

Now it is covered in gray.

The den has a glass door. The den has many windows. It is beautiful outside. The backyard looks like a snow globe instead of a small field with a thin tree and a wooden fence. The backyard is proof the house is not alone.

Dad tries to open the glass door, but it is locked. He goes to unlock it, but it is already unlocked. *There must be another lock on the outside*, he thinks.

Dad hammers the glass. Behind the glass is more glass, more backyard. Behind more backyard is a mirror. Behind the mirror is mirror. Dad stares at himself in the mirror. He does not like the looks of the man who glares back at him.

Dad climbs the stairs to smash a window in his bedroom. He does not make it to the second staircase. Grandma stops him on the ground floor. She has become a Slip n' Slide. He knows the Slip n' Slide is Grandma instead of an ordinary Slip n' Slide. Her face lies at the end of the plastic sheet. It is now giant, plastic, dead. Her enormous mouth is opened to accommodate Slip n' Sliders. It is fun to slide into a dead grandmother's mouth. It is fun rather than deadly because Grandma's mouth is plastic and dead and Slip n' Sliders can pick themselves up after they slide into her mouth and do it all over again.

Dad is surprised Grandma has turned into a Slip n' Slide. It overwhelms his ability to tell his family there is no outside, only mirror.

The Slip n' Slide is slippery with water. The brothers consider slipping and sliding. Paul decides against it. Slipping and sliding is against the rules of the living room.

Matt takes off his shirt and pants. Mom tries to scold him but burps come out instead of words. There are little cars on Matt's boxer shorts. He and the cars slip and slide into his grandmother's mouth. He lies on his stomach, enjoying the sensation of the water on his skin.

Mom says to Dad, "Please remove our son from my mother."

Dad says, "Let him be, Helen. He is mourning the loss of his grandmother by lying down in her mouth. It is perfectly healthy."

"He is disobeying the rules of my household."

"There is no rule against using a Slip n' Slide indoors."

"Some rules have existed since the creation of the Earth. They do not need to come out of my mouth. They have always existed. There has always been a rule against using a Slip n' Slide indoors. There has always been a rule against lying down in the mouth of a dead relative."

"Is it against the rules for a dead relative to transform herself into a Slip n' Slide?"

"Yes, but she cannot be punished. She is beyond punishment. The dead cannot go to their rooms and think about what they have done. Going to rooms and thinking is a burden of the living." She walks over to Matt. She bends down to tap him on the shoulder. "Young man, go to your room to think about what you have done."

Matt complies.

Dad remembers something important. "Oh, I forgot. We cannot leave the house. We are trapped. There is no outside, only inside. It is all room. Wall. Mirror."

777

M att likes his room. It is the greatest room in the house. He likes getting punished. He gets punished a lot. He would rather spend time with his room than time with his family. His room has a cable TV, DVD player, video-game console, CD player, laptop computer with wireless internet, bed, window. Matt wishes he never had to leave his room. It makes him feel safe. Nothing is boring when he is in his room. Everything is boring when he is outside. As he walks up the stairs, Matt wonders what would happen if he committed mass murder. Would he never have to leave his room again? Mom's punishment would be severe. But what if a tornado tore off the walls and his flesh? *She would probably let me leave*, he thinks. It is difficult to live without flesh. Matt does not have the constitution to succeed. The dead are exempt from punishment. Not leaving his room until he dies from lack of flesh is appealing to Matt, but not as appealing as never leaving. He does not know if mass murder is worth it. It would involve many sleepless nights.

Matt walks into his room, closes the door. Where is his cable TV? Where is his DVD player?

19

Where is his video-game console? Where is his CD player? Where is his laptop computer? Where is his bed? Where is his window?

Who has replaced these objects with empty cardboard boxes?

Matt abandons thoughts of climbing a watchtower with a rifle.

He tries to open the door. It has become a cardboard box. He flips out. He massacres the cardboard boxes with his feet. He is like Godzilla.

Matt's feet feel funny. He does not know why.

This is the reason why: His feet have become cardboard boxes.

This is the reason why he does not know why his feet feel funny: His eyes have become cardboard boxes.

Mom and Paul do not know what he means when Dad tells them it is all mirror, and he leaves them to smash a window in his bedroom. There is something wrong with his bedroom. It is different. Everything in the house is different.

It is no longer his bedroom. It is now also his wife's bedroom. It has not been also his wife's bedroom for a long time. Since The Great Schism. The arguments over small things. His sons do not know he and his wife have been sleeping in separate bedrooms. His sons have not heard of The Great Schism. He and his wife conspired to keep it a secret. They continued to live in the same house for their children's sake. This would have been impossible if they kept sharing the same bedroom. There were no extra rooms for one of them to move into. Dad hired a carpenter to build a wall in the middle of their bedroom, in the middle of their bed. They told their children they were too old to enter their bedroom. The conspiracy was successful. It did not make them happy, but it was easier to cope with their disappointments.

Now the room has been rewound, but he and

has wife have not been rewound. This will inconvenience them.

Dad pushes the mattress forward. He considers the panic button.

999

Years before The Great Schism, Paul had an encounter with the panic button. He was babysitting, watching the Softcore Pornography Channel while his brother slept. He liked the act of watching softcore pornography more than the pornography itself. He was able to access it with his parents' illegal cable box. He liked how the box opened the gate to the scrambled world. The scrambled world was visible from any room in the world, but could only be entered through his parents' bedroom. He liked to enter worlds that were choosy about who they let inside. He liked to become a part of a hidden place. He liked secrets, to be absorbed by a secret.

The panic button was a secret.

It was not there, then it was there, behind his parents' mattress. He did not know it was for panicking. Just for pushing. He pushed, expecting to be absorbed by a secret. The burglar alarm filled his ears with pain. He did not know the code to turn it off. He called his parents at their friends' house. It was difficult to hear the code. It was difficult to hear the secret word he would have to tell the man who called him on the phone. It was difficult to hear the knocking at the door. But it frightened him. He went downstairs and peeked through the curtains. A man with a flashlight stalked through the front yard. He waited for the man to go away, then punched the code into the console. The alarm went off. The phone rang. He answered, said, "Flamingo." His brother continued to sleep. His parents came home. His father pushed the panic button again. The alarm went off. His father pushed the code in the console, answered the phone, said, "Flamingo." Paul did not understand why his father had pushed the button a second time. His brother continued to sleep.

101010

Dad considers the panic button. It seems like a good time to push a button designated for panicking. Will a man with a flashlight knock on the front door until there is a front door, until the outside is outside rather than mirror? Or will the room fast-forward to when it was two rooms and pause before things stopped making sense. Never pressing PLAY.

Dad pushes the panic button.

111111

It becomes quieter than quiet. The walls ceilings floors fold into themselves and sink into the dirt. The outside is outside, not mirror. Dad floats, looks down at Mom and Paul. They also float, but not as high as Dad. He searches for Matt, does not find him. Matt is a cardboard box.

A man with a flashlight knocks on his head. Dad says, "Please stop that."

The man stops after a few minutes, looks around, shines the flashlight into Dad's eyes.

It is still light out. The beam is cruel, unnecessary. The man with the flashlight is underdressed. Nude in a snowstorm.

Dad walks over to where the window is supposed to be. He punches his fist at where the outside is supposed to be. It makes a sound of bondage, hurts his knuckles.

The phone rings. He answers. The woman at the end of the wire asks for the password. Dad wants to tell her about being trapped in the house. "There was no outside," he would say, "but now there is an outside, but it does not matter because the outside has taken us prisoner." Instead of telling the woman at the end of the wire these things, he says, "Esophagus." He did not mean to say, "Esophagus." It is as if someone has taken control of his mouth.

The woman at the end of the wire says, "Thank you." The quieter than quiet ends. The walls ceilings floors rise from the ground, reconstruct his home. He is no longer floating or able to see his wife, son, or cardboard box. He is confused. "Esophagus" is not the password. He is not sure what it is besides an organ that transports food from his neck to his stomach.

121212

Mom and Paul are hugging. This is what Mom does to cope when she is under stress. Paul does not get any benefits from hugs. He is doing it to comply with his mother's desire.

Mom's consciousness drips out of her ear. Crawls up her son's shoulder, into his left nostril. It has a milky consistency.

Mom's consciousness enters its son's brain, has a fistfight with his consciousness. Mom's consciousness shows its superiority over his consciousness, which leaves his brain out of shame. Having no brain to inhabit, Paul's consciousness enters his mother's brain.

Mom and Paul are startled about the locations of their consciousnesses. They stop hugging. They stare at each other, trying to convince themselves they are looking into mirrors with reflections that do not follow instructions.

Dad comes down the stairs, enters the living room. He grabs his wife's arm, says, "Come with me."

Paul's consciousness decides to comply. Otherwise it would experience pain from resisting Dad. Paul's consciousness allows Dad to lead it toward its parents' bedroom.

They walk into the room. Dad closes the door. He initiates what he does to cope when he is under stress: he takes off his clothes and his wife's clothes, maneuvers their bodies onto the bed, manipulates his member into uprightness. He has done this ever since Mom has been his wife, even after The Great Schism, although it was with less frequency and more anger.

As Dad enters and leaves his wife's body, Paul's consciousness yells, "Dad! It's me!"

Dad does not understand the words leaving his wife's mouth. He thinks they are an indication of the pleasure she feels.

Paul's consciousness goes numb to survive its father's thrusts.

A couple of minutes pass and the consciousness feels a wetness and it is over. Dad rolls over, says, "I love you, Helen."

Paul's consciousness says, "It's me, Dad."

Dad says, "I know it is you. But why are you calling me Dad? That is unusual."

"You're my dad, Dad. I'm Paul. I don't know how it happened, but I'm inside Mom. It's like a bad movie."

Dad does not believe Paul's consciousness. He says, "That is ridiculous." He only believes things he can see, feel, touch, smell. He thinks his wife is seeking retribution against him for initiating his coping strategy after The Great Schism.

Paul's consciousness feels bad about losing his virginity to his father, being penetrated rather than penetrating.

131313

Matt is a cardboard box.

141414

Dad is angry at his wife for seeking retribution against him. Naked, he gets out of bed, leaves the room, slams the door. He stands on the chair underneath the attic.

Dad is the only family member who has been in the attic. He has warned his wife and sons not to go up there. "The floor is filled with holes. You need to know where to step or you will fall. I know where to step. I will never fall." Dad sometimes brings things up to the attic. These are things his family does not need but feels bad about throwing out. He relocates the items so his family will never suspect the attic is anything but a storage space. He relocates these items so his second family can have objects that remind them of their existence. Some fathers escape to the movies after having loud arguments with their wives; Dad relocates items to the attic and spends the night with his conflict-free backup family.

Dad opens the attic door, pulls himself inside. His conflict-free family is waiting for him. His conflict-free wife is named Detritus. His conflict-free children are named Ion and Polarity.

Dad sits down at the backup kitchen table with his children. Backup Mom serves meatloaf. Dad eats the meatloaf. It is delicious, conflict-free. He talks about his day with his backup family. He embellishes a little. He does not mention how there is something wrong with the house. There is nothing wrong with the attic. It is perfect. He tells his backup family lies about how he went for a morning bicycle ride. His backup family does not know about the snowstorm. They do not know it is winter. They do not go outdoors. The attic is perfect. Dad does not want to leave. As long as the attic is perfect, he will never leave.

161616

Paul's consciousness lies in bed. In his room he seeks knowledge. He searches for the means to cope with the experience of losing his virginity to his father while inhabiting his mom's body. He traces the walls with his eyes. He starts at the closet, goes above a painting of a bicyclist, over the door, throughout the ceiling, turns left until he gets to his wall of bookshelves. Tracing the walls with his eyes usually has a calming effect. He does a lot of tracing. He is often stressed. But he has never been *this* stressed, so the tracing does not have a calming effect. It has a frustration effect.

Paul's consciousness gets out of bed. He walks toward his wall of bookshelves, wraps his arms around a row of books, flings them down. He experiences a calming sensation. He does the same thing to another row. Another row. It feels good. He looks down. The floor is covered with books. He likes throwing books on the floor, but does not like picking up after himself. This is why he does not throw books as often as he traces walls. He turns to another shelf. This time, he pulls books out one by one and drops them on the floor. He pulls out a book called *Cellular Metabolism at Fifty Degrees Celsius*. A secret passage opens in the wall.

The designer of the wall of bookshelves thought no one would want to read a book that sounded so boring. The designer of the library has never been inside Paul's room. He has never been inside anywhere. He loves nature. The secret passage leads into a womb. After a secret-passage seeker is ready to leave the womb, he will exit the womb. The exit of the womb is located in a place that is different from Paul's room. It is a place where the secret-passage seeker has always wanted to live. The location of the place is different for each secret-passage seeker. When a secret-passage seeker enters a secret passage, they choose to leave a place they dislike for a place they assume they will like. But there is no returning to the old place if they do not like the new. There is no book called *Cellular Metabolism at Fifty Degrees Celsius* in the new place. There are no books there that open secret passages.

171717

Paul's consciousness walks through the secret
passage.

181818

The living room feels bloated. It has eaten too many microwaveable dinners. It never gets a chance to exercise. It would like to hike up a mountain or get a membership to a fitness club. But it cannot do these things. It would be impossible. It would take the living room one million years to walk to a fitness club. The world would end before the living room got into shape. The living room feels bloated.

Mom's consciousness feels her son's chest, throat, elbow. She is fascinated. She feels underneath his armpit. There is a latch. She opens it. A door opens in her son's armpit. She peeks through. The living room thinks she is smelling her son's armpit. She sees the house's laundry room.

191919

Mom and Dad will try to sell their house after their sons move out. The real estate ad will list four bedrooms. But there are only three bedrooms. They will try to pass off the laundry room as a fourth bedroom. But it is not a bedroom. It is a laundry room. It is dark and dank and there is a crawlspace behind the dryer. *But it is carpeted,* Mom and Dad will think, *so why couldn't it be a bedroom? You can just take out the washing machine and the dryer and pretend there isn't a crawlspace and put in a bed and you'd be set.*

A realtor will show the room to a potential buyer. The man will say, "This is not a bedroom. This is a laundry room." The realtor will say, "Look closer. This is a bedroom." The potential buyer will look behind the dryer. He will get on his hands and knees. He will crawl into the crawlspace. He will look for the bedroom. He will crawl for the next thirty years. His body will hit a wall at the end of the crawlspace and he will suffer a brain aneurysm. Mom and Dad will never sell their house. They probably should not have listed the extra bedroom.

202020

Mom's consciousness gets an urge to do the laundry.

Matt is a cardboard box. He wonders what is inside his mass. Organs veins bones? Emptiness? A toaster oven?

He tries to turn his head and look inside himself. Fails. He has no head. He does not know how a cardboard box can see, but he cannot see inside himself. *If I had hands*, he thinks, *I would tear myself open and wait for something to spill out. I would not cry.*

He pushes himself to the closet, but cannot open it.

He writes on himself with sharpie pen until it reads:

Matt's Closet
25 Spruce Lane
Syosset, NY 11791

He pushes himself down the stairs, toward the front door. It is still missing.

The wall where the door used to be gives birth to a new front door.

The newborn opens itself for Matt, who crawls onto the front steps and remains.

A postal worker picks him up, takes him to a mail processing plant where he is processed, picks him up again, delivers him to the inside of his closet.

222222

The front door ages, retires, and dies, leaving behind a severed doorknob. It is an antique.

232323

Matt is a cardboard box. He relaxes in his closet. He likes being in his closet. There are secret things his family does not know about like dead frogs and empty cans of silly string. He likes keeping secrets from them.

There is a small hole in the wall of his closet. This is his favorite hole in the world. It is a gateway to his brother's closet, which has always been restricted to him because he is not a flying mouse. He regrets his decision to become a cardboard box instead of a flying mouse. He stares down into the darkness of the hole. This is where he stores the things that bring him shame. He drops them into the darkness, into a place where they can never shame him again, unless he excavates the wall where the hole lives. He will not be able to begin the excavation anytime soon. He is a cardboard box.

Dad reads Ion a bedtime story. It is about an elephant who lives in the city.

Eli the Elephant is the only elephant living in the city besides a few zoo elephants. The inhabitants of the city are human. It is not the type of city that is inhabited by talking animals. Eli is almost ordinary, except he lives in a city instead of a cage or the jungle. He is too big for a house, so he often blocks traffic. The city council are always shouting, "Eli the Elephant is a scourge to our way of life!" He does not know he is an inconvenience. He likes living in the city. He likes blocking traffic. No one is going to tell him he cannot live in the city and block traffic. Well, actually, they tell him this, a lot. But he cannot understand what they are saying. He speaks in roars and trombone-like bellows, not English. He likes people, especially when they are speaking to him in their silly language. Their silly language makes him laugh until he spits water out of his trunk and onto their faces. The looks on their faces make him happy to be alive. This bedtime story is about the U.S. Army and how the U.S. Army are trying to end Eli's stay in the city with tanks and automatic weapons and helicopters that drop ouchie things. Eli likes people, but he does not like the U.S. Army. He does not like living in the city with them. He does not like it when the U.S. Army fills him with bullets. He does not like it when he dies from being filled with bullets.

252525

Dad did not intend for Eli to be filled with bullets. The words just slipped out. He meant to say Eli made friends with the U.S. Army and went ice skating with them. Ion says, "Daddy, I don't want Eli to die!" He cries. A tear hits the floor and the attic folds like a beer can that a beefy drunk has smashed with his forehead.

The attic has lost its perfection.

262626

Paul's consciousness is jumping on a bouncy castle. He has always wanted to live in a bouncy castle. Actually the castle is bouncy, but not a castle. The castle is his house, but bouncy. It is a nicer place to live. His house lacked joy. The bouncy castle house is filled with joy. There is no joy without the ability to bounce from one room to another. Bouncing enhances quality of life. Walking deteriorates it. Substitute bouncing for walking and there is joy. Paul's consciousness cannot stop smiling. It hurts his mother's face a little, but he does not mind. He is willing to suffer the ramifications of joy. There cannot be joy without pain. Paul's consciousness is the sole inhabitant of the bouncy castle house. No Mom Dad Matt enhances his quality of life. Other people's quality of lives would deteriorate without family, but Paul's consciousness prefers a house free from volume. Mom and Dad's mouths have high volumes. They have long conversations from different rooms. Matt walks tastes touches smells and Paul's consciousness is unsatisfied. With bouncing and solitude, there is joy. Paul's consciousness bounces through the beginning of the bouncy castle house to the end. It hurts to smile. But the discomfort makes him smile wider.

272727

Matt is not a cardboard box. Matt is Matt. This is a new development. Once he was a cardboard box, now he is Matt. This is the way things happen sometimes. There does not always need to be a reason for an alteration. Things have the capability to change on their own.

Matt is disappointed with being Matt. He wishes he were a flying mouse. If he were a flying mouse, he would be able to access his brother's closet. But he is not a flying mouse, so he must find an alternate gateway. He tries to make the closet hole larger by headbutting it. He does not succeed. It is too painful. He tries to make a gateway with his fists. After twenty-six punches, he decorates piles of clothes with his blood. He stops punching. He stops decorating piles of clothes with his blood. It is against Mom's rules to decorate clothes with blood. He is a rebel, but now is not the time for rebellion. He tries his knees. He hammers the wall surrounding the hole with a knee. The wall shatters. Wallflakes rain down on him. He brushes them out of his hair and steps through the expanded hole and into his brother's closet.

The closet has no clothes to bleed on. Its shelves are empty. Coat hangers hang from its rack. Miniature closets hang from the hangers. Matt opens one of the miniatures, revealing more hanging closets. He tries to open Paul's closet door. He cannot wrap his hands around the doorknob. The doorknob is not for humans. It is for cardboard boxes. It cannot be turned with human fingers, only box edges. As Matt struggles with the doorknob, he wishes he were still a cardboard box.

282828

Mom's consciousness is doing laundry. She is separating the whites from the colors, the machine-wash colds from the hots, the mysterious from the easily untangled. She puts a pair of boxer shorts resembling her current trapped-in-her-house predicament into one pile, a sock that reminds her to devote time to personal hygiene into another. She puts her son's body in a third pile, considers whether she should start with the whites, the colors, or the fleshed. Washing a predicament will not cleanse it of its stains. She does not have stain stick. She cannot go out for a stain stick. There is no front door. She decides to wash the fleshed.

She opens the lid, maneuvers her son's body inside, chooses the warm wash option, presses the button to start the cycle, closes the lid making sure to avoid impact with her son's face. The warm water pours through the sides of the machine. It feels nice on her son's clothes, on her son's skin. She relaxes, but then the water level is so high she has trouble breathing. The center of the machine moves back and forth. This is unpleasant. This makes it even more difficult to breathe. She wonders if her son will be upset with her if his body is no longer capable of sustaining his consciousness. The waves crash into his face and the surfer of suffocation hangs ten into his nose cavity.

292929

Dad thinks, *I am a good man, a good father. I must do the right thing. They only deserve the best. Where there is no perfection, there is no value. When there is no value, the only option is to end their suffering. I am a good man, a good father.*

303030

Paul's consciousness bounces. Matt rips through the closet door. The bouncy castle house deflates. Paul's consciousness stops smiling. He is furious. He looks at his brother furiously. He bounces furiously, relishing the last moments of fun he will have in the place he has always wanted to live. The bouncy castle house becomes a mat that you can walk on for a mile while wiping your feet. Matt stands silently. Paul's consciousness says, "What are you doing in the place where I always wanted to live? This is my place where I always wanted to live, not yours. You have ruined everything. I hate you. You are a bad brother. My quality of life declined the moment you were born. I wish you had tumbled out of another woman's womb. I hate you and wish you were born dead."

Matt stares at his mother's body, says, "Mom?"

313131

Dad crawls into Polarity's designated area, pulls a teddy bear from his arms, puts it over his head, presses it down hard. Polarity struggles. Dad kisses his hairdo and whispers, "I am doing this because I love you." Detritus crawls into Polarity's designated area, screams. Dad stops smothering Polarity, goes over to Detritus, thrusts his index fingers and thumbs through her eye sockets until they meet her brain, pulls. Gray matter falls out on the attic floor. He goes back to Polarity, finishes the job. Walks over to Ion's blanket and pillows. Squeezes him until he explodes like a piñata. Candy organs spill out of his remains. Dad cries and eats the candy organs. While he is crying and eating, his body crashes through the floor.

Mom's consciousness wakes up in an open coffin with Grandma. It is a large coffin so it can accommodate Grandma's status as a Slip n' Slide. She considers celebrating her existence with a round of slip and sliding, but it is against her rules. If she does not obey her rules, they will lose their oppressive power.

Mom's consciousness peeks over the side of the coffin. She has never been inside this room. Life-size cardboard cutouts of her family are dangling from the ceiling by coat hangers. Below her family sit sad people. She does not know them. None of them resemble any person who has crossed her path in life. They are unique, funny, strange looking. Mom's consciousness begins to climb out of the coffin. The mourners get out of their seats. They say, "The dead must remain in their coffin while the ride is in progress." They take their unique, funny, strange-looking hands and push her back inside. The coffin rolls off its pedestal and onto a rollercoaster track. Mom's consciousness does not like roller coasters. The coffin propels itself forward, up, upside down, up, down, diagonally, forward, up, upside down, up, down, and diagonally. Mom's consciousness does not like traveling in all these different directions. She whispers to herself, "People were not made to go upside down. The benefits of upside down are impossible to determine." The coffin goes up again. It smashes through the ceiling and the cardboard family cutouts rain down on the mourners' heads.

Mom, why do you hate me and wish I were born dead?

I'm not your mother. I'm your brother. You have destroyed the place where I have always wanted to live.

That's weird. Why do you want to live on a sheet of plastic?

It's not a sheet of plastic. It was once our house in the form of a bouncy castle.

Bouncy castles are awesome! But they get boring after I jump on them for a few minutes and scare away all the little kids with my acrobatic skills. Why have you always wanted to live in a place that gets boring so fast?

I wish you were born dead.

No, seriously. Why?

It's more fun to bounce than to walk. I'm tired of walking. If walking were a person, I would kill him. Kill him. Fucking kill him. I would pour gasoline on him, light a match, and put him out just so I can do it again and again and again until he earns the death fucking earns it he's gotta earn his death before I let him go to the place where personifications of walking go after I fucking kill

them.
Whoa, Mom. Calm down.
I'm not Mom. I'm Paul.
You look a lot like Mom to me.
Something happened.
What?
Something.
You're not making any sense.
It doesn't make sense to me either.
I don't believe you about not being Mom.
I don't care.

Dad lands in Mom's consciousness's coffin. She sees Dad's bloody hands, his backup family's bodies. The roller coaster falls, crashes through the floor of Mom's consciousness's funeral, smacks on hard cement in a dingy basement.

Dad looks at his hands, says, "I did not do it."

Mom's consciousness looks at the basement. She looks at a flat-screen TV. She looks at a Playstation console. She looks at toys. She looks at games. She looks at the cold, concrete floor. She says, "But we don't have a basement."

Dad stares at his hands, says, "My family murdered themselves. It was the right thing to do. I am proud of them. They are extremely skilled at self-murder. They would be extremely wealthy if they worked as hired self-killers. I swear to God this is the truth."

Mom's consciousness says, "We did not murder ourselves."

Dad says, "I am aware. My other, better, more-loved family murdered themselves. I swear to God this is the truth."

The mourners peek down from the hole in the

ceiling.

Mom's consciousness says, "You don't have another family. I would have known if you did. I am very observant. It is difficult to hide an entire family."

Dad says, "I kept them in the attic. They were happy there until they chose to do the right thing. I used to visit them after having arguments with your mom. Before I had a second, better, more-loved family I would go to the movies to stifle my anger. But that is expensive. It was less expensive to hide a second family in our attic, a better, more-loved family capable of stifling my anger."

Mom's consciousness says, "I am very upset. I am upset you were cheating on our family with another. I am upset you have killed them. I am upset you have broken the rules of this household. I do not allow people to live in our attic, particularly if they are my husband's unauthorized secondary family."

Dad is confused, says, "My husband's?"

Mom's consciousness ignores her husband's confusion. "Even though we are separated, emotionally, adultery is not allowed when we continue to live inside the same walls. You must exit the premises at your earliest convenience.

Dad looks around the basement. There is no exit. There is no earliest convenience.

"I do not allow killing under my roof. I will never be able to wash the blood off the floor. You will never be able to wash the blood off your hands."

Dad scrubs his hands on the stone, mortared walls. He is not able to wash the blood off. The scrubbing results in the sprouting of more blood, his blood, which mixes with the blood of his surrogate family.

Mom's consciousness says, "I do not allow lying. The truth will keep us together. Lies will draw and quarter our bones until our pieces reside in different counties. It is extremely painful, and this is why I do not allow lying."

Dad says, "I do not care about your rules and I do not care about you." He violently removes her shoes, socks, and tickles her feet until she screams and says, "I feel a sense of completeness and I don't know why."

Matt and Paul's consciousnesses hear the screams of their mother's consciousness. They trample out of Paul's room, over the hallway, into the direction of the screams. The sounds escape from the back of a painting done by a man paralyzed from the neck down. The canvas contains lip impressions combined to form the shape of arms and legs. Matt removes the painting from the wall, revealing a zebra-shaped hole. Paul's consciousness points to the hole, says, "You go first."

Matt says, "No, you go first. You're the parental unit. If something happens to you, your sacrifice will probably ensure my continued existence."

"I'm not Mom!"

"I think this whole 'I'm not Mom!' thing is an elaborate ruse to get me to go into the terrifying tunnel first and you've known about the terrifying tunnel since the day I was born."

"Shut up, stupid," Paul's consciousness says, pushing Matt into the tunnel.

The terrifying tunnel has existed before the Andersen's house was built on top of a swamp, before the town planner decided to build a suburban neighborhood on top of a swamp, before white people set foot on North America, before there were stars in the sky, before random chance resulted in the creation of matter. The terrifying tunnel has always been here and it was formed out of nothingness when nothingness was feeling bored and wanted stuff to do at night to pass the time until it became substantial.

373737

Matt's face smashes into the ground of the terrible tunnel. He bites his tongue and tastes cotton candy. The edible cotton spills out of his wound and overwhelms his mouth, making it difficult to breath. He gasps for air and a dark shadow gorges itself on the cotton until he's able to breathe again, then crawls down his throat. Matt gets up, composes himself. Paul's consciousness meets him in the tunnel, looks around, sees the walls covered in unreceived valentines, removes one, reads it, finds out it is a valentine for him from a girl who he had a big crush on in seventh grade. She died in an automobile accident on her way to school that morning. They never said a word to each other. His body trembles. He finds it difficult to cope. He takes a deep breath, breathes in the terrible tunnel's stale air, and helps his brother up.

Matt has a tickle in his throat. It is the dark shadow sliding down his pharynx, pretending it is a kindergartener on a playground. Then onto the stomach. It hurtles down into his rectum.

Matt shits himself. He removes his jeans, his boxer shorts. The dark shadow leaps out of the bowel movement with a smile, ready to do it all over again. It leaps up and Matt closes his mouth. The dark shadow smacks into his lips, falls down, looks disgruntled, as if Matt has taken away its childhood. There is now a shit stain on Matt's lips. He rejects the soiled boxer shorts, puts on his jeans, stomps on the dark shadow until it is a violet smear on the floor, walks further. Paul's consciousness follows.

383838

Mom's consciousness and Dad are pro wrestling. No matter what they do to each other, they do not feel pain. Mom's consciousness unplugs the television set, carries it to the top of the couch, jumps off, and smashes her husband's face into the center of the screen. She then knees him in the testicles fifty times while calling him TV Head before each attack. Dad does not feel like he has a head. He does not feel like he has testicles. He feels nothing. The guilt from killing his replacement family has washed away. He is not happy. He is not sad.

Dad removes his head from the television set. He places it carefully on the TV stand. Plugs it back in. Detaches his son's head from his body. Pushes the POWER button.

Paul's face lights up in the glow of America's Funniest Home Videos. It sweats, burns, gets crispy, blinks its eyes, explodes. Bits and pieces fly. They fly and attach themselves to Dad's new corduroy shirt.

Paul's torso stumbles over to Dad, removes the bits and pieces, scatters them onto the floor, starts with a small piece and rolls it over the other bits.

And pieces. Rolls them over the other bits and pieces until it forms a ball. A ball that resembles a head, somewhat. Mom's consciousness places the ball that resembles a head, somewhat, onto her son's neck. She does a handstand. Her son's head does not fall off. She says, "I feel relieved." She lunges at Dad. Throws him into the wall. Tries to make the wall absorb his bones. Does a good job, but is not quite there.

Matt and Paul's consciousness enter the basement. They say, "MomPaul! What are you doing to Dad?"

Mom's consciousness stops trying to make the wall absorb her husband's bones. She feels ashamed.

393939

Why is there a basement in our house?

Am I adopted?

Why does my head resemble a ball that resembles a head, somewhat?

Do you still love me?

Why don't you love me anymore?

Can I have my body back?

What were you trying to accomplish by feeding Dad to a solid object?

Who do you love more? Me or Matt?

404040

Mom's consciousness says, "I love you both the same."

Paul's consciousness makes a game show buzzer sound, says in an Alex Trebek-like voice, "I am sorry, but that is not the correct answer." Says in a Paul Andersen-like voice, "Things are different now. Changes have been made. Your rules have become obsolete. The only laws that exist in our household were voted into legislation by truth and beauty."

Mom's consciousness says, "Your question is an assault, an assault on me as a parent. It is unfair to ask a question when lies are prohibited and the truth will crush hearts and vertebra. You are a cruel child. You are cruel and I wish my birth canal had been vacated by either a football or a pogo stick rather than a cruel lump named Paul. I will not dignify your question with a response. It would be an undignified response, and I am a dignified lady."

Dad flees from the center of the wall. He has no regrets. He says, "Paul, if you are actually Paul and not your mother although the possibility is inexplicable to me. Paul, Paul, Paul, Paul, if you listen late at night, you can hear your mother shouting into my ear, 'I love Matt more than Paul. He is my perfect child. Paul was my former test subject. I raised him to formulate strategies in parenting. What to implement and what to avoid to achieve perfection. In summary, Matt is my favorite child'."

Mom's consciousness tries to make the wall absorb Dad's bones for the second time.

414141

Please stop pushing me into the wall.

Stop your lies.

They are not lies. They are the truth.

Psss. It might be the ruthtay, but I don't want to hurt Aulpay's feelings even though I only ovelay him a little.

Mom, you are whispering really loud. Mom, I can understand Pig Latin. Mom, let's hug for the last time so I never have to itch your varicose veins again.

424242

Mom's consciousness hugs Paul's consciousness. Paul's consciousness squirms. Mom's consciousness exhales regret. The consciousnesses await the exchange. There is no exchange, only transformation.

Paul's body becomes Mom and Dad's private bathroom. Mom's consciousness feels at peace. She turns on her shower, lets the water sprinkle across her tiled floor. She has never felt such a connection to her house. It is a sense of completeness even more fulfilling than the fullness of a basement.

Mom's body becomes the attic. Paul takes comfort in its secrets, stores objects that delight, removes those that repel.

Matt tremors. He becomes the living room. His ceiling pets the grandmother. He lives. For the first time, the living room lives.

Dad becomes the front door. He walks through the hallway, plants himself into the wall, opens himself. Everything is now outside. The mirrors have gone to the realm of dreams.

The house on Spruce Lane goes to sleep, wakes up, undergoes hygienic rituals, leaves through the front door, goes to work, goes to school, goes for a walk, mourns its dead, eats pizza at an Italian restaurant, continues its daily routines, goes home, eats dinner with itself, lives, exists.

About the Author

Bradley Sands is the author of Sorry I Ruined Your Orgy, Dodgeball High, and others. He has an MFA in Writing and Poetics from Naropa University. He lives in Boston, where he sometimes eats pretzels.

www.ingramcontent.com/pod-product-compliance
Lightning Source LLC
Chambersburg PA
CBHW071201130626
46555CB00004B/1540